As If a Bird Flew By Me

As If a Bird Flew By Me

SARA GREENSLIT

Steve —
May your days be
filled with song —
Infinite thanks —
Sara

FC2
TUSCALOOSA

The University of Alabama Press
Tuscaloosa, Alabama 35487-0380

First edition

Published by FC2, an imprint of The University of Alabama Press, with support provided by the Publishing Program at the University of Houston–Victoria.

Address all editorial inquiries to: Fiction Collective Two, University of Houston–Victoria, School of Arts and Sciences, Victoria, TX 77901-5731

Cover and book design: Lou Robinson
Typefaces: Janson and Commerce
Produced and printed in the United States of America

The paper on which this book is printed meets the minimum requirements of American National Standard for Information Sciences—Permanence of Paper for Printed Library Materials, ANSI Z39.48–1984

Library of Congress Cataloging-in-Publication Data

Greenslit, Sara, 1970–
As if a bird flew by me : a novel / Sara Greenslit. —1st ed.
p. cm.
ISBN 978-1-57366-164-5 (pbk. : alk. paper) —ISBN 978-1-57366-828-6 (electronic)
1. Women—Fiction. 2. Violoncellists—Fiction. 3. Psychological fiction. 4. Musical fiction. I. Title.
PS3607.R465A93 2011
813'.6—dc22

2010053744

Without Sue,
without the Greenslits and the Bengtsons—
everything fades, everything falters—

The tradition of 'ghost opera' is thousands of years old. The performer...has a dialogue between past and future, spirit and nature...The 'little girl' holds tiny bells and sings the lament of the 'little cabbage,' a little girl who has lost her parents. Such an old, sad song, it's the essence of ghosting. You can talk to the past, the stone can talk to the violin, and the cabbage can sing of her sorrowful life...

Tan Dun, composer (b. 1957 in Hunan)

CONTENTS

Blackbird 1
The Cellist 3
Celia Cracks Open a Door 7
Migrations: Close Range 11
Our Histories (Are Blurring) 13
What Is Known, As It Is Written 19
Blackbird 23
Something to Fill in Our Hours 25
Give Me a Broom 27
Migrations: Of Locks and Dams 29
Animal and Verb: Celia's Other Lists 31
Of Radios and People 35
Later Generations 37
A Sound You Want to Fall Into 41
An Old Story 45
Celia Dreams of Ann 47
Maps 49
Crow Out the Cellist's Window 53
Migrations: A Ferocity and Beauty You Can Almost Touch 55
It's in the Vowels 57
Celia Listens for a Blackbird 59
Reversal, No Fortune 61
Questions from the Spoken to the Unspoken World 63
Migrations: One Very Large, Unexpected Guest 65
Ergot or Not 67

Ancestor, Stranger, Here = Then 69
Notes Towards A 73
Celia Considers Her Options 77
Migrations: The Temptation of the Transoceanic 79
We All Stem from the Fragments of Others 81
Ann Speaks 99
What's Lost, What's Found 101
At the Precipice of the Held Note 103
Migrations: #7804 105
It's Not Clear If It's a Rift or a Rising 107
The World Within 115
That Blue in the Periphery 117
Petition 119
Blackbird Sky 121
Sources 125

The following excerpts appeared in these publications in slightly different forms:

"Notes Towards A" *Action, Yes!*, 2010
"Our Histories (Are Blurring)," *Gone Lawn*, 2010
One paragraph excerpt in Mud Luscious Press' "Stamp Stories," distributed via Starcherone Press, 2010
"Celia Dreams of Ann," "Something to Fill in Our Hours," "An Old Story," *Western Humanities Review*, 2010

As If a Bird Flew By Me

BLACKBIRD

The sky is a trampoline, a gasp, a dream. It's here and there and in between. It's my life and yours. It's particle and wave. It's thick, it's thin. It's breath and exhale, it's countless lungs filling. It's molecule and pollution, warmth and chill.

Falling fully splendored, the air catches a blackbird. The bird rises, the ground dropping away to sky and up, the wind exalted, above. A salty tide pulls from the shore. The bird has a tiny heart, beating, its scaled feet clutched behind it, shadowed by its body, and it keeps with the upsurge, the stars in their daylight slumber.

It shrees from every tall place it can find—shrubs, cattails, bridges. Surround it with openness and it will call and spit and sing out the day.

There's certain beauty in what it is, in its name—red-winged blackbird, four strong beats, a song to the world. Here is the winged and the red and the black. And it is not alone. The flocks mottle the marsh with their earmarked territories. To call is simple. To fly is better. Give up and go into the grace of sky.

THE CELLIST

As if the songs had tarried in her hands, notes held in her tendons, phrasing in her bones—hibernating for a decade, bars upon bars upon bars of Bach, of minor key meanderings, now set loose, unbound from their muscular recesses.

The elasticity vanished, her first and fourth fingers cannot reach an octave, cannot claim surety in finger position or fluidity of the bow. But the vibrato, the sure slide into a harmonic, home as the open low C. That is all still there.

The more she plays, retuning her ear with scales, the more her fingers elongate. Her second finger and thumb find each other, remembering, parallel through the cello's neck—yes F, yes C, yes B flat, yes E flat—yes CGDA—up and up—the other fingers fill around the second finger with octaves and fifths and fourths—and her ear still knows the moment when strings glide into tune, the overlapping vibration clearing into one line: A = 440 Hz. There is a mystery clinging in her, her sternum pressed against where the cello neck meets its back, and the thrum of chords enters her, her skin, muscle, bone, heart. Her blood sends the song she is improvising to each capillary, so that music latches onto erythrocytes, hemoglobin and note now soldered and circulating, now adding with each bow stroke, each breath. The notes saturate the house, push through glass into the winter street, through the neighbors' windows, and she wonders, What can they hear? A shy pause, and then she places the horsehair against the strings again, and the room heats with unleashed years of phrase and motion, her hands pouring out what she had forgotten. She has created a new love from the exothermic rendering of song.

—ᴧᴧᴧ—

It seemed that songs were always coming from the windows of her house as a child. Her brother on his trombone in his basement bedroom, she on the cello up in the high ceilinged living room, her sister on her violin in the study. The mahogany grand piano with ivory keys—from the grandmother she never met— *All of it, all of us,* all of the music framed by the large windows and the lake, the lake of the bluest hours.

I want to say we loved it, loved the instruments we held, the hours of scales and arpeggios, the sonatas and concertos, the repetitious circle of practice. I cannot enter the heart of my siblings. I can barely enter mine.

Two hours a day, every day. She has no clear idea of the total number of hours she gathered in her hands and fingers over the years, in her dining room chair turned to face the large room, metal music stand unfolded in front of her, the pages upright and open. A blur of stemmed notes and rests. *Da capo.*

I close my eyes and sift through those I remember learning: Boccharini, Fauré, Shostakovich, and of course Bach, lovely Bach. Who else? The else I forget. I could go up to the cold attic, find and open the box of stored sheets of music, the books of agility and tone exercises. But I won't. Not yet. A fair and grand catalog of emotion rests in that box. I cannot muster my muscles to do as I say. Not yet.

She can almost remember the cello line from *Scheherazade.* Sit her in the audience and her left hand will grab the notes off the invisible cello's neck. Her right hand knows the weight and proper drag of the bow, the speed lent by horsehair across four strings.

My hands remember, too, the first phrasings from Bach's Cello Suite No. 1. The arpeggios, bow cascading across G, D, A, the harmonious chord made if all three strings were sung together.

(all morning her dog has followed the sun across the oak floors)

Her hands are tired. Pinkie and first fingers from stretching to find and hold the notes on the fingerboard, from gripping the bow as it moves across the strings. Whatever songs she improvised, the energies of her muscles override with aching. Catalog the hours past, the hours of her teenage years, the back of the cello firm against her sternum—*I should have paid more attention to the shift of light. By hour, by season.* She did not get lost in her instrument then. *I was not one of those kids who closed their eyes while playing, and swayed. No, I was a tense pillar concentrating so that I did not make a mistake.* The others, her friends, were tuned into some other, unreachable station. She knew it. She was not possessed by what seemed to enter them. What otherworldly vestibule they must have entered when they began to play. *No, I did not have that.*

Between that and now, over ten years of not playing, the case gathering dust and guilt. But she would never call herself an ex-cellist. Nor cellist on holiday. It was more of a hiatus, a break in the arc of expectation. More of a gestation or chrysalis-time, a span where she explored the world's other myriad forms of music. And what songs she carried within her, songs never shared, unexplored—

Hour by hour, note by note, a spun yarn of organized noise:

scale up, scale down. Major. Minor. Chromatic. *Sweets I was not gathering.* She was collecting accuracy under fire and repetition. Looking back, now she thinks those notes held grace too: not just the crescendo and swell in Barber's "Adagio for Strings" or Bach's long, first, exquisite note in "Air in G" or the discordant and sonorous Respighi's "Pines of Rome." Adieu sweet tune. *Of course I knew not where I walked.*

Yet so, she wishes she had known and played Górecki, Tavener, Arvo Pärt. She has always been the dark and moody one, the one who preferred the slow and minor-keyed, the subterranean ecstatic—

So what is it like, then, to play from within a section of 12 cellos, an orchestra of a hundred? *Lean closer. I shall whisper it to you. It is a cathedral of the colors of the world, translucent and energetic, pushing aside all other sound, so that you are swimming in and lit with it. It is your bones vibrating, your heart about to burst. You are contained by your skin, but you have flown from your core. You are a field of poppies opening. You are a plane taking off. You are infinity and history. You are a star flaring. Sound comes from you and around you, layered harmonious, spectacular gleanings—*

How so many dark marks on a page become such uncontained, pulsating necessity—

CELIA CRACKS OPEN A DOOR

She begins to think of herself as Celia, a newness to wear, to inhabit—because, surely, there is another person with her same birth name out there, in New England perhaps, where a segment of the family tree landed. But Celia? She cannot think of any family member with that title. The soft C of Celia and the S of her real name overlap, and she is satisfied.

And so she begins to talk about herself in third person: "This is Celia calling, leaving a message... Celia will see you later."

She imagines the future, some other person speaking of her, and in that future, she would only exist in third person: "She called herself Celia..." As if by speaking in this point of view now, she is preparing herself to gently accept that she will become the past. (All the *I*'s in daily speech wearing her down, insulating her from unpredicted intimacies and blurrings—the geese returning, a lover's eyelashes, cumulus giving way to stratus.)

—~—

She is thinking about roots—sun, tree, ax, boards, chisel, cello, song. Mother, daughter, piano, *adagio* and *rondo*. Birth. The slow escalation towards desire, a wanting tongue, empty hands, that first kiss: Girl, gather me up.

Mouth, music, notes from which a chord is built, such a note occurring as a triad, or as another song into the sternum.

—∞—

Celia watches from her living room a woman and a dog walk by. Sometimes it's the same woman, the same dog, and a man, sometimes the same dog with the man, no woman. She thinks they must be her neighbors, carving a repeated and invisible arc around the block, the dog marking the identical trees, bushes, lampposts each day, just to make sure all the other canines who pass by get a chance to get caught up on what's happening.

She wonders more and more, as she strains to hear a cellist out her window, is it one of them?

Celia starts to make up names for the trio. One day, it's the Bland Noun Day: Dog, Woman, Man. The next, Texture Day: Fuzzy-Sweater, Beard-Shadow, Irresistibly Brown. Another: Everyone's Covered in a Fine Mist. On the days she misses their passage by the house, she feels a little less complete, a little wobblier in the world.

—∞—

She has a shoebox from her father of sepia-toned photos of 19th century family members, the cardboard backings soft around the edges, wearing away. The women with the small waists, standing next to their seated husbands in their wedding pictures. The men who don't smile, who part their thin hair to the side, oil it down. Her great grandfather's shoes are scuffed. His mustache is tidy.

She makes a short list of dates, important only to her tiny dot on the map:

1685: Bach is born.

1886: my great great (paternal) Aunt Sadie, my namesake, who lived to be 103, who lived from the end of slavery to right before the moon landing, received a small leather bible with a lock. Holy Bible, Translated from the Original Tongues. She was 21.

1989: I graduate from high school and wear my dead (maternal) grandmother's high school ring, 1929.

1992: I graduate from college. I was 21, nearly 22. It's 300 years after the Salem executions, of the hanging of Ann Pudeator.

Pudeator being her relative, you can count back the generations,

Genealogy fever, a found Christmas letter from 1968
stating that there were 14 generations back to the Mayflower =
16,384 people in the family tree. Letter signed off,
"Let us leave you with Teddy Roosevelt's trite statement—
'Thank God for the iron in the blood of our fathers.'"

Pudeator's first husband had same last name as Celia. She's not a genealogist, just merely curious how one goes from there to here—like how flat stones skip across calm water if you do it right. She so often does it wrong.

She gently touches the faces of the dead in the pictures with her finger. She traces their noses, their high brows, the lines from their necks down their arms. *From this to here*, she says out loud. From this, to here.

MIGRATIONS

Close Range

Almost a mirage: 8:30 a.m., Highway 13, north, near Lake Superior, a wolf in the road, stopped. He or she was thin and young and not nearly afraid enough of people and what cars do to animals standing in the street. It lifted its huge floppy feet into the wet grass and stared— She gasped, her heart flared, and the wolf wobbled—and its look was one of almost recognition, but mostly a half-distrust. It saunter-wavered back onto the highway and walked down the middle and another car was coming and she flashed her truck's headlights and the approaching car barely slowed, the wolf unswerving from its stance on the yellow dotted lines, and two more cars came, too fast, tailgating, almost clipping him as he stood on the margin now, then he got back onto the pavement, looking back at her hardly breathing, looking back, and he took the corner, and was gone.

OUR HISTORIES (ARE BLURRING)

How far away can you hear a carriage coming down a dirt road?

How long to fray the edge of a petticoat?

What happens if you get caught singing at home, alone?

Is that rage calling across the marsh?

—∾—

The air is thick with the dead. Outside, a lamppost casts a corridor of light into a winter night. Alive, we shine in that beam, oblivious of what waits just beyond it, its inhabitants sliding through our very breath. The night is gargantuan, expanding, taking the heat of our bodies.

—∾—

Time as a variable, as a line, a continuum, a circle, a start and stop, fast-forward, relative, keepsake, period, waste, matter of, once upon a, piece, ordinary.

The last leaves on trees move in the breeze stiff and fast, vibrating like plants in time-lapse photography.

—~—

Palm to a horse's shoulder, skin twitching under your touch—how long can you hold it there? Your hand smells like a hayed field—

They don't like to be ridden, she said. *Once out of the view of the house, I get down and the horse follows me like a large dog, reins in my hand. I know they don't want a rider—look how they linger and shuffle and eat along the trail, and look how they speed back to the barn—*

The ball of the foot in the stirrups, sweat on the saddle, ankles to the cage of ribs, heel scraping the keyboard of bones, the cinched strap

Can you hear a carriage a mile away? The hooves and leather straps, the metal bit?

Fetlock, withers, croup, poll—

Brown and black canterings across green fields

—~—

If you have a close family, when you die you may become a person with a rich history. You are lucky and will be remembered with stories from your life, whether they are true, exaggerated or fabricated.

Less fortunate are those who only have a few close relatives or friends to consider them. Either way, you may be reduced to a brief anecdote, repeated, so that you become the words, and your life, your body, and the remainder of its hours never existed. Likewise, if you are famous, you may become one thing: what you did that one day (or days) that the world kept your name.

Further down the scale are those whose names are known, but have no narrative. What happened along the way from daily activity and interaction, to this?

If you are lost, quiet in a large family, next generations will have no idea who you are. If you tend to be this kind of person, write your name on the backs of your photos.

Then there are those who have no stories and no names—everything is engulfed into the past, into carbon and vapor.

If you are childless, your history will be omitted by gene and mouth—who will send words out about your life if not your progeny?

—᠁—

The sky grey, post-rain, the trees are glowing, leafless, a sandy pink to the swaying limbs. It's dense, humid, ubiquitous. The black walnuts reflect the sun, a warbler pulses by the tall congregation, fly, flew, gone, body tapering into thrust wings, a blink, off. The sun, in its setting, yellowing everything vertical, keeps pushing into the bark, into the palomino sky that is gradually bluing, the bark warming briefly. On this spring afternoon, the world is tree, wet road, bird, mossy sky.

—᠁—

A photo in a box of others: a sunburned row of farmers with their seated and stout wives, none smiling

Red beard of her father's father, her strawberry-blond hair as a child

Her grandmother's purse snapping open—*here, a few coins, for whatever you want*

Her grandmother in her elegant wedding dress, skirt tuliping over her lap, her collarbones exposed, a small stone necklace to her throat, silk mary janes each with a ribbon strap and a button clasp— What happened to her elegant dresses after she married?

—ᴡ—

I am five, holding my Siamese kitten against my chest, looking down at her. I am wearing red mittens with a white stripe at the wrist, a red wool tartan hat and coat. Behind me, a snowy hill—our steep driveway? My hair is redder than it is now. My nose looks the same—I would know it anywhere. The cat is struggling to free herself from my arms, sitting up, claws out, blue eyes looking straight ahead. It is around my birthday—a kitten from my parents.

In this picture, amongst the evergreens and snow, I can't say what I am looking for—

—ᴡ—

The spinning wheel whirring, a mixture of lull and repetition (hum, thrum, lie down)—a near jittery loss of self (become the sound and motion, fall into the path of the wheel—)

Can barely hear, far off, the clank of the cow's bell down by the stream

The shadows of small birds traipse past the windows in clumps and single speed—

You might catch me daydreaming—

—~—

Once, once before there were words, there was breath waiting, waiting for words, waiting for mouths about to shape sounds, the guttural, the mellifluous, the fired, the singing, the countless combinations of what will be said. Speak.

WHAT IS KNOWN, AS IT IS WRITTEN

Celia starts to dig around letters, books. She ferrets out probable timelines, truths and rumors. She likes a good list. This is what she finds:

Between 1622-1627: Ann is born in England; or is it 1617? according to one source, with the last name Poynter.

1642: Thomas Greenslade, Ann's future husband, sailed from Devonshire, England (b. 1626) to Salem, Massachusetts—seeking religious freedom?

1848: Ann, married, became Mr. and Mrs. Thomas Greenslade: five children: Thomas, Ruth, John, James, Samuel.

1674: When Thomas Sr. died, Ann (destitute?) was hired by John Pudeator, a wealthy Salem blacksmith, as a nurse to his, some say, alcoholic wife.

1675: Pudeator's wife died.

1676: Pudeator, 20 years her senior, married Ann.

1682: Pudeator died, leaving to Ann two parcels of land, two houses, and 1,300 pounds, and bequeathed money to his five stepchildren. Pudeator will's stated, with the Greenslade name changed: "John Greenslit and to the other fore of my wife's children, viz. Thomas, Ruth, Samuel and James Greenslit 5 pound each." (Or was it a sloppy town clerk who mis-transcribed John Pudeator's will contents? No uniform spelling for four?) Previously, the Greenslit children's father's will named them Greenslade.

Now a wealthy widow with property, with a profession, in a small village—

Ann continued to nurse after Pudeator's death.

May 12, 1692: Ann arrested for witchcraft.

"and Lady, fail not."

Jailed until June 19, 1692.

July 2, 1692: Ann was rearrested for witchcraft.

> *Dorcas Good, also part of the trials but not related to Ann, was accused and imprisoned at age four. Her younger sibling, recorded as Infant Good, died in jail. Her mother,*

Sarah Good, was hanged on July 19, 1692. Dorcas was released on bail after her mother's death. She later went insane.

(None of the twenty persons executed in Salem confessed to having made a compact with the Devil. Admission, though, granted freedom.)

September 22, 1692, Ann was hanged at Gallows Hill along with seven others—Martha Corey, Margaret Scott, Mary Easty, Alice Parker, Wilmott Redd, Samuel Wardwell, and Mary Parker. She was in her seventies? This was last of the executions for witchcraft in Salem.

She types up the list, prints it, and puts it in her purse, so that the history can leach a little into the atmosphere, into the fabric and seams of the bag. She doesn't know what to do with the information. She doesn't even know what to believe, muddlers of historical truth abound. She thinks that she's one of the muddlers muddling right this very minute.

BLACKBIRD

There is no room for dreaming here. Here blackbirds fill the summer with flashing and open wings, spread tails. Above them, planes. Around them, the occasional boater, the tractor in the hay field, cars along the causeway. But they don't mind. They see past that, focus on what's theirs, the patches of reedy greenery and all the hours eternal.

And in the fall, the blackbirds remain when so many others leave for warmth. Forgoing the miles or the terror, they stay and they talk their way through winter. They're here in all their feathery selves, and somehow, they survive as it snows and the landscape empties and night brings out its own cold demons from the shallows of the ocean. The blackbirds inhabit winter, but kept hidden in the trees, buffered from the dark shapes in the air, most make it out the other side into spring.

SOMETHING TO FILL IN OUR HOURS

The losses can be large or small, they can be ragged, they can be deep. A step toward love, a step away. Human or animal, human as animal. When it had been simple. Or perhaps it was.

Of being in this world, then not. A whisper, a brush, a tug to the sleeve. Sun in the eyes. An exhale.

How long can we *never mind* and still persist, without disintegration? Not saying when, where.

Amidst this, the swirl, the cycle of seasons, of days, the insistence of forward, the pull towards the future—there's a gap, a pause, a rift in the cement, the hemline, a crack in the plaster. And beyond?

I was never much in this world. How easy it is to forget you have a body. (Desire made manifest: the passing figure on the sidewalk, the sun in her hair, hand to the dog's taut leash—)

Once inside the mind, there is no end.

GIVE ME A BROOM

WS Nevins, 19th century historian: the concept that witches fly on brooms may be traced to Ann Pudeator.

His proof:
1. 16 year old witness, Ann Putnam:

that ann pudeatar: tould har that she flu by aman in the neight in to a hous

2. Witness, Samuel Pickworth:

I this deponant was coming along salim strete btween ann pudeaters hous and Captin higison hous. it being in the evening: and I this deponant saw awoman: neare Captin higisonn Cornar. the which I sopposed to be ann Pudeatar. and in a moment of time she pasid by me as swifte as if a burd flue by me and I saw said woman goo in to ann Pudeat [eat] ers hous

Nevins: "It was too bad that the woman credited with supernatural powers could not fly away from her cruel fate."

MIGRATIONS
Of Locks and Dams

In 1994-1995, a manatee became the most well-traveled of his species: Chessie, named after the Chesapeake Bay, swam from Florida all the way up the east coast, past the Statue of Liberty, to Rhode Island. By those in charge of such matters, his behavior was deemed in opposition to his survival, so he was captured, flown to Florida and released near the Kennedy Space Center. (Manatees tend to migrate farther north than they used to. Man-made thermal discharges into coastal waters extend the species' range northward.) In 2001, Chessie was sighted again, photographed in a set of locks in Virginia, waiting for them to open so he could go south: "It was clear from the animal's behavior that it had been through these or similar lock systems before," said the photographer.

How she knew it was Chessie and not some other intrepid, wily manatee-adventurer was by the animal's pattern of boat propeller scars: a distinctive long, gray mark on his back, with several small white spots apparent within the scar. "Since then," said the photographer/biologist, "Chessie has also acquired tail mutilations as well, but these scars are not severe."

ANIMAL AND VERB

Celia's Other Lists

How to juice a pomegranate: roll the fruit on a hard surface with your hand, cut a hole in the end, and then squeeze.

Animals as verbs: porpoise, flounder, bear, steer, bug, rat, inchworm, wolf, fish, badger, snake, ram, dog, (flamingo/flamenco).

Bones loose from the body

Pinion & pinyon/piñon

Plover & pluvial

Humpback whales create a circular net of bubbles to trap their prey, krill

Bird songs cascade from trees like falling fireworks, like the many thin limbs of a willow tree

The good parts, the soothers and lovers, of ourselves

Coniferous & carnivorous
Prosimian & persimmon

Coots on a lake, pointillists in their own painting

How my dog knew when we saw the wolf along the highway shoulder that it was no mere dog

A flock of sparrows regrouping and swirling at dusk above a pink stucco house

Liebchen & confusion
Dendrites & saprophytes

Animal extinct from the Midwest by WWII: lynx, cougar, marten, elk, wolf, grizzly, passenger pigeons—

A scattered flock of crows, the birds up and off the tree, left, right. It was as if someone's essence had alighted just then, splitting as it rose— Could this be how we depart, flocked yet singular, birds huddled around a pile of seed, then startled into the trees?

Containing birds and dirt and blooms, oxygen and breath and blood

I miss my microscope, pond water eye, green twirling, being

Mistaken road i.d.:

1. porcupine	or	tufted grass clump
2. deer carcass	or	burlap
3. broken glass	or	petals from a flowering X tree
4. mouse	or	blowing, tumbling leaf
5. sideways-walking ghost crab	or	ibid.
6. top hat	or	tire fragment
7. raccoon	or	sod
8. splayed red organs	or	loosely coiled rope
9. frog jumping	or	a fluttering plastic ant trap, rolling

X is a star and Y is a polished stone, X is a leaf, Y is a stem, X the sun, Y a freckle.

Like an octopus trying to fit through a dime-sized hole (it gets through ok)

Mandolin & pangolin
Pleonasm & neoplasm

A small child, crawling, could fit through the gigantic aorta of a blue whale (its heart, the size of a VW bug).

Two crows flying above and along the road, one shifts in front of my moving car, as if pulling it along with its body—the bird coasts, dips, beats its wings once, rises, coasts again, exactly the speed of my vehicle, me following the bird to a destination as if in a fairy tale—

Saturnine & sanguine
Veracity & mendacity

Mola mola, the ten-foot diameter sunfish, sun themselves sideways in the water, and wave their small pectoral fins to attract gulls to eat their parasites.

Abandon me! But leave me a single swallow
And another. And one more…

Falling asleep while watching dragonflies fill the yard and hunt mosquitos in the open sunset, the lake behind

Lieder, liter & lighter
Lyre & liar

A jay's feathers have no color—light's pyrotechnics, all shimmer and blur, reflection of wavelengths of blue

Trilobite to tricuspid, bivalve to bicep

A crow leaves the electric line by falling, wings barely open to catch it, before the first wing beat, the caught breath of *If*—

OF RADIOS AND PEOPLE

The rhythm of the commute, jazz on the car radio, a regular snare beat—the same tempo as the gait of the girl crossing at the light, matched to the hazards of the stalled Mercedes in the turn lane, to the exact downbeat of the limp of the older man looking down to the sidewalk, hands clasped behind his back. The trumpet's amblings intertwined with a woman walking, her hair set free from her hat and grazing her shoulders, sprung along with tempo and line, the cadence of the setting sun, a trumpet pulling the beat out of each of us, out of inanimate objects, out to those who don't know they are listening (trumpet echoing, underwater the guitar tumbles, feedback backtalk—)

LATER GENERATIONS

Celia can't help but notice how many *Johns* fill her family tree. *I could draw a filial line back to 1692, but she starts with the closer relatives—my uncle, his son/my cousin, my cousin's son, my grandfather, my great-grandfather, my great-great-grandfather, my great-great-great-grandfather. Add "great," multiply the superlative, keep digging—*

Is the 300 year dot-to-dot of Johns a ridiculous loss of vision? Or is it stability steeped in the Puritan tradition of passing names down, "transcending death through progeny," *and thou shall honour your father?* [and mother]?

And yet she knows so little about her mother's side of the family, except how her maternal grandparents died—grandfather: heart attack, grandmother: metastatic colon cancer.

—~—

On October 24, 1693, Ann Pudeator's son John, a year after her death, is lost at sea while fishing off Salem. His wife Abigail remarries six days later.

Celia starts to wonder,

At what point did we not have to remarry in a week?

And for some reason, she also wonders: *At what point in evolution did animals get souls?*

—~—

Names are written on the back of the pictures in the shoebox, probably by her dead, paternal grandmother, after whom she named her newest cat. Her father only laughed and shrugged. The writing on the photos is in blue ink, formal, slanted to the right, a little wavering—does age unsteady a hand like this?

—∿—

She cannot fathom this: the billions of people, all the living and the dead, each individual with loves and tics and gestures, no two alike— How to grasp the energies and desires and selfhood of so many?

Maybe this utter deluge of heartbeats is what keeps her inside some days, the too-much-ness of the world, the gravity of the living mixed with the dead.

I find it difficult to exhale completely, the air packed with the careening and intersecting spheres of sentience—

—∿—

And then there is Revolutionary War *John:* his and his wife's graves were lost over the years to prairie grass, unmarked and unknown until 1974 (the search, part of the bicentennial fervor).

—∿—

Tendrils far and wide: she finds in a *New Yorker*, from 1954:

> "...blood ties to a surgeon general of Colonial troops in the Revolutionary War, with a lieutenant under Miles Standish, a casualty at the Battle of Quebec in the French and Indian

War, and with an ensign who was a charter member of the Ancient and Honorable Artillery Company of Massachusetts, the first military company in America."

What she thinks about as she reads this is, *They still use the same font.*

In the article, one of the relatives even claims to even have found a signer of the Magna Carta. The Magna Carta? *I mean, come on, people.*

A SOUND YOU WANT TO FALL INTO

Now the cello was purely hers. No teacher, all of her sheet music packed in an attic box. She had just her search for what the cello wanted, an exploration of what it could do if asked.

She craved Bach, her worn and oversized copy of his six cello suites, her teacher's finger notations on the page. But for now she lets the box rest in the attic for a little bit longer, so that she can dream through the dusty and luminous box, where like a notebook's blank page, everything was possible. She just had to begin. And to trust her hands.

She never loved the cello like this as a child—she knew hours of scales and impatience, the cat under her feet, and she knew sloppy indifference. She never improvised, but merely stuck to the printed notes in front of her. The cello was what other people had written.

—∿∿—

Even at work, she thinks of her cello, locked in its velvet-lined case, the potential energy in the pegs, the strings taut, vibrato from past shimmerings still trapped in the wood's atomic bonds.

The cello has no label, no maker's mark, but she was told by a refurbisher that it was German, over 100 years old, and the front and back had been overly planed inside, so now they were thin as a viola. That was why the cello was so loud.

Musicians describe instruments as sounding warm, and she finds this adjective murky. A timbre you want stumble into or lie down in? That reminds you of oncoming sleep? A welcoming door? Yes, her cello is all these things, but a little brighter, more insistent.

She knows a played string instrument is a happy and healthy one. If live music in a hospital can speed healing and decrease pain, then that same music must surely maintain the instrument's own health, vitality and personality. Like a Turkish rug salesman once said to her in Soho, "To hang a rug on the wall is to kill it." And she once said at a party, "An unplayed cello is a cello that taunts you from its corner." She knows what it's capable of.

Some of the instrument's top edges just barely meet the ribs, and a crack near the tailpiece is always threatening to unglue. A wolf—a buzz that sounds only when a certain tone is played, the A in second position on the D string in hers—arrives each winter. Winter, too, has the strings rising (or is it, the fingerboard falling?) so it is harder to play just one string at a time and not brush the others with the bow. The bridge is a bit warped, as is its spare that recently resurfaced in a tin marked *Cat Treats*, mixed with shells and a vertebra of a fish she found on a beach in South Carolina.

—∾—

She stretches out her fingers on her left hand, tendons and muscles taut, and her reach is abridged, fumbling. Fifteen years ago she practiced two hours a day, and what ease notes rolled from her hands then. Now, stiff and out of tune, she plays an almost unrecognizable scale, her ears flinching at the missed notes, her fingers' memory clouded.

—∾—

In high school, she was friends with a prodigy—a violinist, composer, pianist. He practiced six hours a day, attended a special school that let him study around his music schedule. He had no special genius sheen to him so that a stranger could pick him out of the crowd. Only a pale and thin countenance, an awkward pause before speaking. It was difficult to make him laugh, and she and her friends wondered what would happen if he couldn't play anymore since he knew nothing else. They were in the same youth orchestra, he the concertmaster year after year, undefeated, and dating his slightly older stand partner, she mid-section (therefore, rank) of cellists. She wanted external proof of his gifts, something she could turn over in her hands, that she could admire but never acquire, that explained the source of his talents. But all she had was his performance and the reportage from his daily life. Nothing else, not a scent on his breath, not a slight limp in his walk, nor an almost discernable aura of electricity that would make the hairs on your arms stand up.

—~—

A scholarship audition at a modern and cavernous concert hall twenty years ago: the unending wave of sound—the only time she'd ever be alone on that stage, she knew, in her life, the hall dark, voluminous and empty, eating her notes— If only she could be there without the panel of judges, startling her to speed and stumble through the "Prelude," Suite No. 1, skidding and knocking through the piece, her hands shaky and cold, a bow pulsing in her unsteady hand. The notes out of tune, her heart thrusting to escape from her body, her eyes on the back of the theater, squinting under the lights. If she could be alone, perhaps then she'd know a glimpse of what so fiercely seduced others.

—~—

It's in the vowels, the held note, sung, the sound you want to fall into—

—~—

She decides to open the box of music from the attic. She is right, the moment she begins to play through her old music, her pulse races at what she has forgotten, everything she lost—the key signatures blur, the notes—is that a 32nd? A 64th? A high B or E? And grace has left her hands—no easiness between notes, her finger hand clumsy and dulled, her bow arm rigid and inconsistent (and always falling behind). The pages bring panic—volumes of scales and arpeggios and harmonics and chord exercises, sheet music to sonatas, encores, concertos, slow recital songs (songs after her own heart, sadness, pensive, out from the horsehair of the bow—)

The pages bring little, how little she still can read and play. The pages bring tears.

After that, she does not touch the cello for weeks.

—~—

What it means to not play. To give it up. She can never say, *Forever*, and so the roots of nagging and craving exist and coexist.

So many things reside right under the surface for her—another whole world of regret, anger, embarrassment, longing, fear, each cross paths, cluttering internal traffic patterns.

In her synapses, the bars and phrases of cello parts from symphonies, short pieces, the spark of improv, all persist, rusty, impossible. Or have the neuronal interconnections been reconfigured to better suit her life as it is today?

AN OLD STORY

It is an old story. Wolf and deer, a chase.

Take this image, the motion, the surprise of the wolf-chased deer, they cross the road/yard/field in a breath, a held breath— a grey and red blurring, slowed in memory—

Catch the eye of the wolf—white sclera, black pupil (inside the uncolor, the earth goes on forever: black pupil held in your own pupil, image flipped upside down by the optic nerve, flipped back up by the brain: Look a wolf in the eye and you'll see—)

There's only one pair of predator and prey, the constant duo of hunger and chase, the two propelled by non-thought, the sphere of *going*, so not to be gone—

No time to pause, the deer hardly notices you, you standing still in jeans and a green sweater, looking at the lake and thinking of bears and berries, or thinking how the great lake could be the ocean, how you sense a whale might breach off the coast in front of you, your Day Mind, saying, Impossible!, you shrugging it off, Slough off, you say— The deer pulls through all of this—the whale disappears, and your mouth forgets the taste of berries or the fear of spotting a bear Sasquatch-tall at the end of the road— No, you have the deer, bristle brown, white flag tail, agile and concentrating on navigating the scrub and pine, zigzagging (who knows the woods better, who mapped this trail more times, wolf or deer? Who is more ladened by parasites, who more thin-ribbed?). How far have you run today?

Was it close—

Or, the deer, a break, then wolf?

Perhaps they burst by and you don't process what is happening until it's over. Or do you know right then? Is it even a word, or more of an intuition, more of a premonition, guttural?

Perhaps you were just down the road, feet up, eyes to a book or eyes to a nap, or eyes on the same water the wolf and deer follow in their periphery, the blue they probably never truly forget, a brisk and cold memory in the bones, a frozen wave in the winter, were you there?

No matter, you have the sight of them, the scent.

Forget about love, forget about food, forget about ever going back to work, you want to stay here, suspended on the edge of the lake surrounded by fern and red clay, bog and hawkweed, the spoor of raccoon and bobcat, a glimpse of the surreptitious.

CELIA DREAMS OF ANN

One of my first memories: my mother wiping her hands on her apron, calling from the back door, the sun low, so I had to squint to see her. Ann? Will you pick out a chicken?

I was eight and liked the chase. I knew once you had them, they quit flailing and let you carry them around the yard like dolls. I liked, too, how they became smaller, my hands in their feathers, their taut bodies a surprise beneath.

I went for a red hen, and she was mine and I held her.

Mother came over and I said, Isn't she beautiful? And then she had the chicken upside-down by its legs and I knew, I knew I had been part of an awful unfolding, my hands already stained with blood.

I stood aside and I understood what Axe meant, and I understood how dinner came to me each night, and there was blood on the stump, the axe on the ground, a severed head and a flapping, released, running body. It was easy.

I was then free to see death everywhere.

No, it was the color I remember. It was the yellow of an evening yet come undone. My mother had her hand to her forehead, I could just see her silhouette, hand up, elbow bent, and her voice, through all the yellow. She wanted me to catch a chicken. I was eight and loved a game.

Once the chicken was in my arms, its kicking stopped and I petted its neck and breast.

Isn't she lovely, Mother?

Loveliness comes with ease when you are eight. I had golden feathers in my hands, and the day was burning away and my mother was cast in light and shadow. Umber, amber, ochre, the sun a topaz, setting.

Yellow chicken, yellow hair, yellow sky. Mmm. I spun. I stopped. I stretched my chicken out to her.

MAPS

"When using any driving directions or map, it's a good idea to do a reality check and make sure the road still exists, watch out for construction, and follow all traffic safety precautions." —maps.yahoo.com

When Celia was a child, she had this heavy, square and glossy book about the countries of the world. Throughout the book, layers of vellum covered pictures of the continents. Lifting layer by layer, you could see who grew wheat, who mined coal, who had boreal or rain forests, who had the most cities with the largest populations. She wonders where the book is now, what cosmic garage sale, start-stop-start-stop, new owner to new owner. If you flattened your palm to the vellum, it was slick and cool, yet ripe with static in the winter.

Tributaries (zoom focus, zoom across the ocean, into each salty bay, riffling reeds—whoosh down the coast) of chance—…—filtering, joining, into making You.

From marsh to strip mall: time line—and don't forget the hundreds of thousands of years as the ocean flooded inland, and then later, it flooded out, each time changing the jigsaw coastline into a new configuration.

And whenever there is not enough air in the house, when there are too few doors, she gets in her car and drives to the nearest wide summer field of wheat, the green current, the inland tide apparent in the wind over the grass. Exhale. There she is less a person of bone and muscle and more one of gas and atom.

She has never driven through Kansas, Nebraska, eastern Colorado, or the Dakotas. *Imagine the sky there*, she thinks. Would the world always seem like an open window? And are the ghosts less apt to stay, because there is less to snag them, like a plastic bag on a tree limb?

—∞—

And what would be the benefit of walking the same path from where the old jail used to exist to Gallows Hill?:

> In 1692, the Salem jail stood on St. Peter Street (then called "Prison Lane") near its intersection with Federal Street. The traditional route taken by the condemned from the jail to Gallows Hill was through St. Peter Street, down Essex Street, and then through Boston Street to the point of its present intersection with Aborn Street, and from there to the summit of Gallows Hill. This roundabout path permitted the least precipitous approach to the brow of the hill.

The world is now paved, the trees razed, house after house after house disappeared. There's a baseball diamond and a water tower at that hill. Now it's a park. Just down the street to the southeast is the Salem Hospital.

And look at the names of the roads near the hill: to the west, Gallows Hill Road and Witch Way. To the north, Putnam and

Boston Streets. The east, Proctor and Pope Streets, Hathorne (the judge), Phelps, Essex, Sewell, and Hawthorne (the author). The Osbornes get a street in Northfields. Few of the accused or convicted have been bequeathed streets. Mostly the accusers and the legal men, and one embarrassed relative who changed the spelling of his name.

Salem, the town of one-way streets.

And then there's the voice out there in the historian crowd that deduced that the cart with the condemned could have never made it up the steep hill, that another, smaller hill was chosen instead.

—ꟿ—

And what of walking those cobblestone streets, pressing your palm into the granite of the witch monument, of tracing with a finger Ann Pudeator's name in the stone?

—ꟿ—

There is a transparency in our hearts, an utter dislocation of will, of sight. You cannot name that tree, that bird, that cloud. Your feet upon the pavement. Close your eyes. Try to discern the passing streets by sound, feel, by pacing. Where are you? Where have you gone?

The morning opens with a low grey sky, a slow, infrequent tumult of sparrows. Only one neighbor so far is awake enough to have driven his car away from here. Even the molecules in the wood fence look still. There is a clock and its numbers. There are lights to illuminate our dawn. You drink a full glass of water, the empty glass is a clear bell. The percussive barks of a dog, then another. Then a quiet street.

—~—

There is a map of veins in your feet as you walk the grid of the streets, above the layers of rock below. Follow the paths of deer through the woods, thin trails, duck your head under the overhanging branches.

Use the ramus of the mandible as a handle. Missing teeth, open alveoli in a line in the bone. The deep canine tooth easily pulls out like a puzzle piece, then slips back in: home. The jaw is small enough to fit across your open palm and fingers. How do calcium's corridors guide you, now?

CROW OUT THE CELLIST'S WINDOW

All autumn, the dead crow hung upside down by one foot, through windstorm and rain, caught by mere fate of branch and ankle, to swing out of reach, macabre, desiccating— We got used to it being there after awhile, so it was a surprise—like the surprise of first seeing it in the tree—when it finally fell, wings and head thrown back, arched by gravity, stiff. Upright, it looked like it was already flying. For one day, crows mobbed the carcass when you stepped near it. Another month on the curb, it relaxed its wings and head, rested. In the street, on the curb, then back to the street. A few more weeks passed. Someone placed the bird in a paper bag, and the crows flooded in—fifty dove, restless and loud. The wind dragged the bag across the road, the bag floated off, leaving the bird behind in a drive. The neighbor ran over it—it's getting even closer to dirt now, now it's flat—and the crow stays, more of a feathered platter each day, the tires of the car revisiting the torso as if to say flight had always been a bad idea.

MIGRATIONS
A Ferocity and Beauty You Can Almost Touch

In August 2004, a young great white shark was accidentally caught by a fishing boat off California. A great white is the holy grail of an aquarium collection, except that the species tends to not thrive in captivity. This shark not only attracted thousands to the Monterey Bay Aquarium, but she surprised all by becoming the longest captive great white, breaking the world record of her predecessor (198 vs. 16 days). In her time in the tank, she grew from five feet, weighing 62 pounds, to six feet, four and half inches, weighing 162 pounds. Even as a juvenile, she still projected that movie-terror/awe of her larger cohorts in the wild (how easily our minds fill in soundtrack and footage). The aquarium wanted to keep her longer, but she killed two of her tank-mates, soupfin sharks, her aggression escalating as she grew larger.

Before she was unleashed back to the bay, they attached a transmitter to her dorsal fin to track her travels. In six months, she swam more than 100 miles off shore, then her transmitter fell off and she vaporized into the blue.

IT'S IN THE VOWELS

Put your headphones on. The singer's voice pours through your ears, and underneath, the instruments' notes—together they create a passage, an entry into the infinite, not only because sound travels out into the universe, but it collapses inwardly, to the maze of sulci and gyri of the brain, through the doors of our synapses, the axonic hallways, into the unknown, to the general question, *How far can we go?*

Forever and ever and ever.

Sound delves into the warren of the mind—and if you shut your eyes while listening to the lead singer holding the vowels in his throat as he counterpoints the guitar, there's a pinprick that's actually gargantuan, that'll let you in, to fall and fall, and you're no longer commuting home on the bus at dusk, you're traversing internally as well as out to the end of space, music the needle pulling you through the darkness.

CELIA LISTENS FOR A BLACKBIRD

I don't believe it was a matter of how much we loved the earth or not. Or how much we loved God. Or why I became a blackbird, and others—hare, bear, frog, flower, heart in another's body. Or plain ghost. It wasn't a matter of the depth of ardor for our spouses, children, or ancestors. It wasn't because we had sinned or thought of sinning.

We had nowhere to go. We had everywhere.

REVERSAL, NO FORTUNE

Most of the Salem witchcraft convictions had been reversed in 1711 (19 hanged, 1 pressed to death)—

> Giles Corey, in his 80's, pressed to death September 19, 1962: it took three days, and he would not confess. It is claimed he said, "More weight," as the sheriff piled boulders on him. Was he trying to atone to his wife for testifying against her, which lead to her execution? And/or was he also aiming to prevent his property being confiscated by the sheriff, his children losing their inheritance?

"*Mr. Sewall S'r I thought good to returne you the Names of severall psons that were Condemned & Executed that not any person or relations appeared in the behalf of for the takeing of the Attainder or for other Expences.*" All but six: Bridget Bishop, Wilmot Redd, Susannah Martin, Alice Parker, Margaret Scott, and Ann Pudeator. Convictions overlooked, families moved away, deaf to the petitions, with financial restitutions that ranged from $35 to $750 each.

—∞—

Representative Walter Judd (R., MN), a direct descendant of Ann Pudeator, wished to clear her name of witchcraft, in the mid-20th century.

The bill was rejected three times:

"One prominent legislator argued we were trying to rewrite history."

Others worried that the Greenslit relatives would try to reclaim Ann's property, confiscated by the Special Court of Oyer and Terminer at her conviction.

Some feared Massachusetts would lose tourist revenue in Salem if the rest of the witches' names were cleared.

One senator felt that if the bill was defeated, Greenslit would continue to fight, bringing the Commonwealth needed publicity.

Another senator stated since the Commonwealth of Massachusetts did not exist in 1692, it was "not accountable for the deeds of the Province of Massachusetts Bay."

After the third defeat, the *New York Post* headline read, "Salem Witches Kept On Broom to Bewitch Tourists."

—~—

In the 1950's, you could get a souvenir license plate that read "Salem, The Witch City."

—~—

Rewritten, the bill passed in 1957. After 15 years of trying, Ann Pudeator, the only one named in the document, "and other persons" were pardoned after 265 years.

QUESTIONS FROM THE SPOKEN TO THE UNSPOKEN WORLD

(the cellist to her husband)

You can place the hot, red flower of a nasturtium on your tongue like a petalled sacrament, you can create cacophony or melody with a stroke of a bow over strings, you can trace the edge of your dog's soft, brown ear— Yet, sometimes, there is a scent on the wind that you can't quite place, that triggers a memory you can't quite discern, and the distance between Here, the place you sit, and There, the drawer in your mind, poorly alphabetized, moted by dust—the distance is beyond any tangible plane. Sometimes the cat appears to see it, the trajectory into the Other. *Nothing* can have shape, fragrance, texture, right? I'm oblivious to most of the world's turning gears. What I know is that the rosehips are burnishing like tiny persimmons, that the geese have begun to line up in their first tentative tendrils, and that the ways that I love you can seem contradictory, and I just don't have the right vocabulary you so greatly deserve, yet I lean into the chasm with you, my dear, the world with its innumerable transactions for joy.

MIGRATIONS

One Very Large, Unexpected Guest

If you were a humpback whale, what would be your reasons for entering San Francisco Bay? Two times, in 1985 and 1990. Maybe one should wonder why one Humphrey (not his real name) chose not to enter the bay on the other years. He was on his way from Mexico to Alaska. Too busy with friends to stop by? Enamored by a new lady? Behind schedule?

Both visits, humans came to help send him out to sea again. The first time, they had to turn him around in the Sacramento River. The second time, he beached himself on some mudflats.

But we humans, we have clever ways to guide the misguided. We made a net of sound, created by a platoon of boats, and banged on pipes to keep him going—from the Japanese fishing technique *okami.* And then like a siren out at sea, a boat, headed to the open ocean, broadcasted sounds of humpbacks about to feed. They played that hungry tune for 50 miles until Humphrey was safe in deeper water. He was clocked at swimming up to 30 mph.

He has only been seen once since 1990, in 1991 near the Farallon Islands. Is he too embarrassed to stop by?

ERGOT OR NOT

er·got n
1. a disease of cereals caused by a parasitic fungus that grows in dense black masses (sclerotia) in the grains of the ear
Latin name: *Claviceps purpurea*
2. the dried sclerotia of an ergot fungus that yield substances used in drugs to treat migraine and to induce uterine contractions in childbirth

From the same substance you can concoct LSD and you can treat the meanest species of headaches. The ergot alkaloids are a funny family.

You can also, if you eat food contaminated by ergot, end up with this resumé: "violent muscle spasms, vomiting, delusions, hallucinations, crawling sensations on the skin." Sound like Salem?

In 1951, the small French town of Pont-Saint-Esprit had a similar rash of behaviors, of which ergot was the cause. But, no witches there.

So then, what about the rainy spring and summer of 1691? Fungus loves that kind of weather.

And what about where the accusers lived? On the western side of Salem village, full of swampy meadows?

The people of Salem, they ate a lot of rye. Grown the winter of 1691-92.

But the summer got dry, and the bewitchments tapered off.

> *At the end of June and the beginning*
> *of July 1692, I think there was more*
> *imagination than ergot. But by that point*
> *in time three people had already been hung,*
> *and the trials had taken a path that people*
> *felt they had to stay on.*

Any votes, then, for sexual repression, dietary deficiency, anxiety over Indian attacks, mass hysteria?

ANCESTOR, STRANGER, HERE = THEN

In a house's history, if you think about all the layers of individuals who have lived there, it is not hard to imagine a few people absorbed unhappiness, due to some dark streak, and chose to never leave. Those who remain, are their timelines stagnant, a day replayed, a glitch in a record? Or do they ride linear time along with the living?

—ꟿ—

And what would I, Celia, have to say to her, Ann, really? Me, a child of gasoline's rule, of fruit in winter, women lovers, no livestock? My family lives in disparate states and does not speak of the past. I am only connected to that time by my name.

Yet—yet, a millisecond, a flicker of something out of the corner of her body, a passing through the chest, an invisible twine moving her hand— And behind those eyes, who is she but DNA that stretches back to the Mayflower, back over the Atlantic? Who has her reins?

Are we just progeny that carries out our forbears' wills? Ancestor as parasite, or are all possible and past worlds expressed in the present, through this body called Me?

Suddenly, I do not know who I am at all.

—ꟿ—

You can't say I didn't try to fit in. But I never feel at home among humans
What mammal are you? What animal?
Out walking with others, something's amiss, their mannerisms foreign, mouths moving incomprehensibly—
I feel apart. As if I am not
Not the same species
Deeper and older than culture, innate, gene and eons of predisposition
The sky's flat, and it ends and drops away

—∾—

Celia finds her mind going into a state of numbness, how easily she falls there, a habit now—not a window, not a leaf or bird to distract her—a continual flatness that hums with agitated boredom. She is afraid to acknowledge her stupor, to make it concrete and ever-present, for she will have to account for wasted hours, days, weeks, months and years, staring, at a ragged loss of how she got here and why she cannot fight the complacent and deadened inertia of being.

—∾—

I am a foreigner who once knew the language, but time has faded that knowledge. Or maybe I never knew it but only nodded, pretending comprehension. I will have to learn to cover up my grand unmoorings.

Do all our gestures and speech barely communicate what we are trying to say? How can we look at each other in the face day after day knowing this?

—∾—

If each person indeed has a protector—a shaft of light, a presence—overlapping threads or rays crisscrossing, trailing behind—how do we account for the largest puppet show, the omniscient and simultaneous care of billions?

—ʍ—

Dinner is cooling. It's been dark for hours. The cat is facing the door. I grow more leadened as I wait. Winter infuses my cells.

What if, by sitting still, a great maw of sadness opens? Will I step away in fear or look right into it?

—ʍ—

We aim to align our hearts. And yet—

NOTES TOWARDS A

I entered the life of the brown forest...
and I was the stars...
and I was the darkness
Outside the stars, I included them, they were part of me.
Robinson Jeffers

An entire forest of longing, an entire coast

You have cells sloughing off you everyday, an eyelash in your tea, long tendrils of hair down the bathtub drain

No, close your eyes. It's better to keep out the blurring and the racing, the fear of losing, of loss, of lost. The tide is high and it's roaring.

I am watching the minutes and they are not a speeding train. My heart elongates flat and thin as a rail-roaded dime. Anxiety like fiber optics faxing and refaxing. Sheer light, sheared. There is no sitting still. Green. Go.

Stapling, coughing, paper shuffling, metal door opening and shutting, swivel chairs on plastic mats—hum of fluorescent lights, of computers, ears ringing, eyes exhausted with screen fatigue, hands on keyboards, down, up, return. Someone walking down the hall jingles change in his pocket. The women here never whistle. They laugh. Here the clock is no friend. The copier creaks each time its lid is lifted—

You add up your nothingnesses and they multiply in front of you, splay like a deck of cards—your turn, what do you have?

Daydream as sport, as easy languish—ease me through a valley of continual boredom—

You will have plenty of time to rehash your flaws, your flailings. You will not be more or less for what you might or might not figure out/unravel.

This dream is azure and filigree. This dream is a mahogany piano playing Rachmaninov.

Double déjà vu: remembered, yet slightly altered, not abridged, but accompanied by another layer, like painting a door (because a brown door can swallow a whole room up), one color right on top of the other, and when chipped, you see all the years of hues below.

A ruby-throated hummingbird heart beats 1,220 beats per minute while in flight. And it eats its weight in nectar each day—three grams, or 1/8th an ounce.

Loosening and shifting, gravel underfoot.

What is this but a de-selection, a loss of acceleration, of choice? The least amount of will, keeping time with others' requests. It's immeasurable, the selfish vs. the selfless. A horse whinnies in the background, no an ambulance, no a baby, no a car's squeaky belts. You can't name all of them, the curses and the gifts, combined, the together and the apart—hand out for a taxi, hand out for your hand.

I can't quite put the pictures away—they unroll pasts that make me flinch because they are unknown yet also mine.

A chickadee *fee-bee* insists on singing through morning rush hour, a noon tornado siren, a street full of rumbling city trucks.

Our paths worn, to and fro, like the children's book with the rowing crow—to and fro, wings on the oars, starless night, splash and creak, shore ahead, the tendril of morning, rest ahead.

Give me your hand through this brutal forest.

Sounds palpable in the mouth

Treatise of bee, and songs for the crepuscular

The temperament of Now

Barred owls	*who cooks for you?*
Rufus-sided towhee	*drink your tea*
Great horned owl	*who's awake? me too*
Song sparrow	*maids maids maids, put on your*
	tea kettle ettle ettle
Red-eyed vireo	*here I am, where are you?*
Ovenbird	*teacher teacher teacher*

What was it that shimmered by in the night, rousing a dog to bark, alert to trespass and passing?

CELIA CONSIDERS HER OPTIONS

Celia considers a road trip:

She still carries the list of historical dates in her purse. A map of 1692 Salem (by WP Upham, 1866) hangs on her office wall (an *O* marks Pudeator's house). She thinks of driving to Massachusetts, to stand in the shade of trees, to stare at a different town than the one she's invented. And why would she go?: the historical placard and engraved markers, the 21st shine to 17th century buildings, the country of website promotions of witch tours? She can only imagine this reason—to see the river, the reeds at the edge of the salt marsh, the ocean, the possibility of a whale fluke offshore, on the horizon.

The dead are with us, within us, under our nails, coursing along our veins, in the lattice of our bones.

Shut your eyes. Notes from an oboe drift and mist in and out of your range of hearing. What next?

Celia considers the cellist:

She loves the sound of her, the woman who walks by her house with her husband and their shepherd. Once at dusk, the lights were on in their living room, and Celia had been wandering around the neighborhood, slowly, meandering, too agitated to go home, too tired to go far. Then she heard scales. Soft C major. She walked toward the sound.

Scales morphed into a rambling, random song, stalled then re-started. Open strings played with fingers on other strings, a vibrating harmonic. A slide, a chord, a pause, a staccato. A long note held, in vibrato.

She saw her then, her back to the large living room window, the outline of the cello's scroll snug to the left side of her head, left hand moving along the fingerboard, the right arm directing the bow.

Breathless, time is absent—

If it had been darker out, she would've stayed longer, sat on the curb, and just listened, her eyes shut, clasping her knees, head down, to blot out the rest of world but the sound of the cello.

—w—

Celia considers the heart's disbelief at one sentient's absence:

The sound of pet tags jingling in her house, her friend's mutt visiting—the leap of the heart, she looks up, her deceased dog expected around the corner. The past catches up with the present and she sighs, a little lost without his red head in her hands. *A hole in the universe the size of his body follows me from room to room.*

MIGRATIONS

The Temptation of the Transoceanic

The longest known migration of any animal? It's the artic tern, a round trip of 20,000 miles per year, from the northern polar ice cap, to the southern one, and back.

One arctic tern, three months after it fledged, flew from the Farne Islands off the British east coast, to Melbourne, Australia, in three months. That's a journey over water of 14,000 miles. Another species, shearwaters, can live long lives, and one Manx shearwater was calculated to have flown five million miles in over 50 years.

Those seabirds, above, feed while on migration, refueling as they fly along. Bar-tailed godwits, however, do not stop to eat. They fly 9,000 miles from the Falkland Islands to Norway, the longest non-stop flight of any bird. They store 55% of their body weight in fat to propel them on their way.

WE ALL STEM FROM THE FRAGMENTS OF OTHERS

I could possibly be fading
Or have something more to gain

Mazzy Star

I've had my own share of me.

The moon at thick sliver—

Open your ears to it. The sound coming from the forest— Add up the hours of exhale. You have to sit still, lean a little in the right direction. Shut your eyes, think of nothing else.

stand Charged with sundry acts of Witchcraft by them
Committed this day Contrary to the Laws of our Sov'r Lord & Lady

You cannot blame her for the verbs and nouns that spilled from others' mouths. They weren't invited, those phrases—the unexpected turn, levity evaporated. Spillage unleashed. Look what damage you've done.

How quickly the heart finds all the body's corners. Deliverer, pulses everywhere.

Five children in 10 years, two dead husbands. She chose midwifery.

Housewife, deputy husband, consort, mother, mistress, neighbor, Christian. *Relict:* widow.

Pebbles and dust. Kick up the road, the voices rise. For years, tides and whispers, feathers and weather. Earful after earful, tongue after tongue   Choir—   Look at the back of your hands—veins rising, freckles surfacing   Goldfinches find a sturdy branch.

did often hear my wife saye that Ann pudeater would not Lett her alone
untill she had killd her By her often pinching & Bruseing
of her Till her Earms & other parts of her Body Looked Black

The world is full of continuous conversations: Now is surrounded by Past, and both are encircled by Forever.

Was I the ivy, reaching? I had lost my voice, lost it into the pebbles and dust of the road.

Embouchure: mouth of a river, mouth of a cannon, mouthpiece of a wind instrument, the shaping of the lips and tongue to that mouthpiece

The North River, the smell of the salt marsh is inescapable. Does water ever leave her view?

my wife did affarm that itt was an pudeater that afflict her
& stood in the Belefe of itt as Long as she Lived

A woman overweight at 40 will live 7.1 years less than a thin one. A slim 40 year old man will live 6.4 years longer than a fat one.

"You can't say I ever forgave them," she'll hear herself say, not knowing anymore what it meant to forgive. Can you take back forgiveness, nullify it? Was it ever forgiveness then, or what was it called instead?

Given enough time, what does one know?

A febrile stoop to pet the cat—it lingers and curls its tail. All thoughts slow: fur purr world: hand to animal.

This witch is your witch, this witch is my witch,
From California to the New York Island,
From the redwood forest to the gulf stream waters,
This witch was made for you and me.

Not remembering which key to sing in

that his Mother did severall tims in har siknis complain
of ann pudeatar of salim the wife of Jacob pudeatar
how she had beewiched har and that she did believe
she would kill har before she had dun

Wondering, wandering between causative and proscriptive

An appeal, a submissive beckoning—a dog paw on the arm, unintended claw marks to the wrist

Fidgeting and leaning, we love, we love—

Quiet as I never was

Lie down.

Dream songs yet unread

Notes towards Future—

A periwinkle waltz, a polka dot choir, crinoline in the orchestra

Mama in the wings—

The dead are all around us.

Looking at the back of the cello, the lines of grain wobble and blend into the next, like tiger's eye, like a hologram—patina right under her palms.

The clear demarcation between brown and black fur on a dog's thigh

We live in a world where damage can arrive through the minute and abbreviated: parts per million, ppm.

I did drive goode pudeatars Cow back from. our Cowes:
and I being all alone: ann pudeatar would Chide me when I Came houm:
for turning the Cow bak: by Reson of which I this deponant
did ConClude said pudeater was a wich

Already, in her first week of life, a baby has her picture taken numerous times by those who love her, new and beautiful. And already these pictures speak of/to a past—although a recent one—a moment, a pose, a gaze frozen and left behind—and yet, somehow the baby's true essence is absent from each and every photo.

Ghost opera, ghost bird (ivory-billed woodpecker). Bird reborn in a swamp, photographed like a specter, outlined in the frame, just barely.

She wants one pure and beautiful thing, a clean object of vision and desire: take this winter field, grasses the color of wheat, the sun spilling across the flattened clumps, the dog happy to cast about in the rushes, nose submerged in various holes. Ignore the traffic streaming by, the sirens, the soda can—not power lines, no houses, no streets—just this wizened, glowing field in winter, a blue sky—

My mouth, round, open, screaming. I sit up in bed. The room's door is ajar, the window open. I feel made of granite, cast, solidified. I dreamt this way for years.

During the quietest part of the day, right before bed, when still, the mind slowing—this is when the other side opens, and the fear reasserts, a rising dislocation over surroundings and people, displacement ahead—

Ann Puddeater hath often: afflicted me:
by biting me pinching me sticking pins in me: & choaking me

Is that panic in its expression, the rearing black horse flashing the white of its eye in Bonheur's *Horse Fair*?

A visit to the doctor, a 20 year prediction of risk factors: an image, a clear, terrible scene of terminal downfall: heart attack, stroke, complications from diabetes.

Wonderful, mysterious coelacanth: here you are both past and present.

What one can learn by walking the same land where ancestors used to live—

"And the fear of you and the dread of you shall be upon every beast of the earth, upon every fowl of the air, and upon that moveth on the earth, and upon all the fishes of the sea; into your hands they are delivered."

att her examination: s'd Puddeater did: afflict me greatly

The subtle demarcation between black and blue—taffeta shifting between hues—what color is it? you can't hold onto it—

1/4 Swedish 1/4 English 3/8 German 1/8 Danish

My long exhale and inhale against your neck sounds like the continuous tide.

The house is losing light and the dog won't take his eyes off her.

she or her Apperition did offer: me the book to sign

How many times did she walk by that hill, those years before it was named for the actions of the misled? (Gallows?)

Sparrows bathe in the dirt, dust aloft from fluttering wings. A cardinal hops the post of the fence, down to the grape vine, down to the ground, bold, slow. A wren on the end of a maple branch, almost fully-leaved—recycling a bubbly song with complete conviction and effort with each round.

The mask darkness takes, a gentle and insidious friend downward, pulled to the floor, the body icing and bruised, words too much effort to utter— She thinks of it as the devil's foot to her chest, the devil's hand to her throat—

Awkwardness arises in endless forms: sit at your desk all day and talk to no one, leave your hat in the house, do not turn on any lights, stare into the fridge but forget that you are hungry, forsake sleep to wait for the moon to leave the room.

A ragged line of Canada geese v-ing—and towards it, a jet, its silver body the same size as the flock and headed right for it. Give up spatial perspective, and the plane gets closer to the birds, closer… then, yes, the aircraft enters right into the flock. Birds do not fall from the sky. The plane passes through. The geese continue in the opposite direction.

"the entire earth is not our temporary appearance, but our genuine human body"

she told me also that she was the caus
of Jno Turners falling off: the cherry tree: to his great: hurt:
& which: amazed him in his head & almost kild him

The butcher the baker the candlestick maker
the widow the midwife the

Her children, silent

Sweet and savory: meat and fruit, syrup and beast, cider and potato—

Crows that survived the summer's brutal tongue (West Nile virus)

There's the world out there (of men and machines), and then there's The World.

If a throat rarely knows singing, does a voice know something is missing?

she told me also: she was the caus of: Jeremiah Neals wifes death

Complete regeneration of all the body's cells takes seven years

Crow in the yellow locks of a leafless willow—

Had I ever looked at a lover like that before? —my hands clasped loosely around her waist, me leaning back a bit to look at her closely and clearly, her eyes a wondrous brown lined by the sun on snow out the window. She was quiet and soft, letting me take in her gaze—

The roil and avalanche of accusations, the roar of evil intent, self-serving and reckless, the shrieking choir, and all those thrusting pointer fingers at the innocent

The savior is song, what specimen, glory—

The stones that fall to the bottom when thrown into the river—

Afraid of the forest, afraid in town, governess of nowhere—

I saw her hurt: Eliz Hubbard: Mary Walcot: & An Putnam

I've stopped seeing the world— I see the unsteadiness, the vanishings, the distance closer than you think—

The crows have started to build their nests, flying with branches in their beaks, straw, gathered from somewhere.

We are only given fragments to form our own truths, our own story. We will never know our past, our ancestors, our future.

the last night she: afflicted: me also: last night: by her wichcrafts

Did they transcribe exactly what was said? (No. Impossible.)

How the universe gives us the Notre Dame cathedral and quack grass, both.

The wing of a falcon, set upon a white page—

How the world goes and goes, regardless of our undertows and/or glorious notes that will lie mostly hidden to those that follow.

"The body is not an object or a noun, but rather a verb"

The delicate arch—a bridge, a foot, a cheek, an ear, the back—of her

The trajectory of a glance, the friction through air of that look of anger or even clear delight, gathering momentum from there to here, where it grazes my face and enters me to do its multitudinous tasks.

An exhale can tell you everything.

A crow uttered a call that was a mix of a mew, a plea, a sung note.

Cell phone 3.0 oz. Chickadee 0.3 oz.

All the songs of the world, not just composed tunes, but spontaneous ditties, bird song, howls, overlapping cricket wings—

And what about the noise from all the car doors opening and shutting at 5 pm? the chain of honks on a highway? the shuffling feet on sidewalks? all the blinking don't walk signs, the chorus of sirens, the blur of train horns? What songs are these?

she kild har husband Puddeater: & his first wife

The spiderwort and sundrops opened one day apart: what mechanism has them so closely timed?

The hiss of the stove, the heft of the plate— How can one not linger over the beauty and intricacy of a single raspberry? And how it opens you to pleasure and sweetness and seed in your mouth—

Crow overhead with ragged wing feathers, as if an animal extracted a frayed piece from its open wing

Another answer, no answer, too many— If we cannot ask her, how will we know, or suppose?

pudeator tould me that she had done damage,
& tould me that she had hurt James Coyes child
takeing itt out of the mothers hand

Bird as packet of energy, restless, vigilant, loquacious

I do not know any of them, those staunch and sunburned faces of farmers and their wives (even my grandparents unrecognized).

The reddened march grasses blowing like fields of inland wheat

Gather, gather, lift and turn, work hard all week, look past what you yearn—

What is it about a reed-lined lake, red-winged blackbirds shreeing from the cattails, cumulus clouds reflected on the water, the hills filled with dense heads of deciduous trees— What is it that settles the roar inside me, so that I feel at home?

she was an instrument of Jno Bests: wifes death

The sensation of seeing your childhood house from above, on a map—how you struggle to grasp the one dimensional representation with your memory of the three dimensional world.

Summer solstice: light but dark, the sun arching slightly towards winter

Tethered to our histories by gene and landscape. Landscape and sense of place: the land within us is the land with out.

"Indeed, if we are deathless,
Where then is randomness, Art's impulse, true disorder?"

Small specks of rain fall onto my bare skin and feel like tingling nerve impulses, as if the whole body was regaining blood after falling asleep.

Crow fledglings have cobalt eyes.

ann pudeatar: tould har that she flu
by aman in the neight in to a hous

The world at 5 am—how quiet and brimmed with expectancy it is—

The train horn is a B-flat layered with something my ear fails to remember.

I stand in front of the mirror and rarely look closely at myself. When I do, I see a stranger.

What draws us back to where we were born—the scent in the air, the angle of sun, familiar foliage, chemical imprinting in blood and bone from the soil, comfort in custom and dialect? What makes us call our birthplace Home?

Goody pudeator tould hir that she went up to mr Corwins house
to bewitch his mare that he should nott goe up
to the farmes to examine the witches

If she shut her eyes in the desk cubicle, she could imagine the manufacturing plant noises that thrummed through the wall were a plane engine, and that she was flying, anywhere but here, her heart beating against her ribs at 10,000 feet:

Always looking at the clock,
continual tick-tock,
hopscotch, hot
to trot— so much swirling,
swarming— the roar of thought,
not like the pounding of horse
hooves, not that, not
at all, but the roar of low-
flying jets, a jettisoning
shock of sound so nothing
else is heard or watched.

Depression always lingering beneath it all, like a handprint in cement, despite being covered by a layer of brilliant snow.

Sometimes the crows sit so quietly in a group, you don't notice they are right overhead.

In spring, startling upon a desiccated orange tabby in a lushly weeded ditch, the carcass's mouth in a grim rictus, body in a half twist, in terminal unrest.

To welcome and take on the abandoned, our hearts larger than we think.

We dance this new, screwy dance, that's ugly and pretty, and we hang on some more.

How young our mothers look in photographs as they hold us, babies. *They are the same age then as we are now.* In their youth they are almost unrecognizable. We have all leapt forward. How much have we forgotten—

How astounding that a thin tube of cells, although supported by rings of cartilage, is the sole pathway of breath, and therefore life—a dark channel of oxygen and exhale sustaining us as we go on oblivious.

5 a.m. cardinal, the 6 a.m. cooper's hawks and chickadees, and crows at every hour

When was it that I stopped trying to catch myself as I fell asleep, the maw of mortality gaining?

The elongation of time at work—acute, painful—what is missed, what is missing

Goody pudeator tould hir that she killed hir husband
by giving him something whereby he fell sick and dyed,
itt was she tould hir about 7 or 10 years since

"Life is one long, fragmented, murky episode.
The fear of all the wasted and empty hours upon me—"

Unable to answer the question: What do you want?

Someone is spelling her name out loud in another cubicle, and her body knows those sounds, that order of letters—it sounds slightly off in a different voice, but it's her name, and she is pulled and surprised by it at the same time.

Would life take a different turn and feel with a different name?

The flexibility and elegance of hydrogen bonds, forming and breaking— the chords of a baroque string fugue, similarly creating beauty in structure, the melody intertwined like chemical bonds assisting a folding protein

Brown grasshopper flying, falling, landing like the winged seed of a maple

In winter, one must stretch to remember or tangibly imagine the lushness of summer. In summer, how winter's subzero days, and still and stunning white are pure fiction.

she had been an ill carriaged woman

In the shower alone, you out in the hall sweeping, I suddenly remember the taste of your mouth, the flavor of your tongue—

Who was I around those old houses, those tidy, gated gardens?

"Think of yourself as the sky, holding the whole universe."

this woman has come to my house pretending kindness

Hold a note, sustain it (low D on the C string, second to lowest possible: enter chest, enter heart, enter femur) —keep pulling the bow, try to draw the tone from within the cello. Slowly fall, into each of the vibrations (the ear hears how many per second?). Grab the clarity and richness there, the gauzy undertones, lush and forgiving, the note keeps ushering you into it— Gather the slow tumble, the echo you will carry with you the rest of the day, the subtext of each sound that leaves your mouth, beginning with a D, drawn by a bow, held by a finger, given and given and given.

she pasid by me as swifte as if a burd flue by me

I forget my histories, the dead

I forget. We forget.

She is suddenly afraid of the time line of her life.

The evening follows the sun, and the crickets begin their metronome song. Fall has arrived extracting the green from everything, red or yellow or brown revealed beneath.

the nurs s'd you are come to late
for my wife grew wors till she dyed:
s'd Pudeater had often threatned my wife

Once and awhile, we are given brackets of silence to carry us forward. The world moves on, yes how it moves, but where you are standing, just this moment, it is still.

The cricket keeps on.

The light is leaving us. Once again.

(What is one thing I understand the most?)

The concept of all the atoms vibrating— Is it how everything is always in flux, is that why we struggle? No wonder I have trouble focusing—the world's blurry (and I'm in it).

Certaine detestable Arts called Witchcraft & Sorceries
Wickedly Mallitiously and felloniously hath used
practised and Exercised
At and within the Township of Salem

What did they call the devil?: the Prince of Air?

What if there are 10 dimensions (me in 10 places at once, or this mug being used by 10 different people simultaneously)— can this, then, account for the Other, the feeling of disassociation, separation, and incompletion, the surreality of reality?

Smile, say the researchers, and after awhile your brain starts to think you're happy and sends out the sweet neurotransmitters that back up that feeling.

When one has the peculiar tendency of continually residing in the future tense, then one loses her body, in a way, to her mind— Fast forward to what date you are considering, the leap and spring of thoughts that catapult and multiply off one another, "what if" their happy mother.

Mary Warren…was and is
Tortured Afflicted Pined Consumed Wasted & Tormented

A stoplight. A patch of blue sky. Snow loud under your boots. Your dog looking back over its shoulder to you—you know these things. The small and immediate, unabridged: Yes, my friend, *Here* is tap tap tapping on your arm, ready, waiting.

She cannot stop her mind from leaning towards seeing the entropic in everything.

Window. Outsider. Inaccessible history. Landscape. Imagined interaction. View.

I never saw the Woman before now

I never saw: the Devils book nor knew that he had one

I never had ointment nor oyl but neats foot oyl
in my hous since my husband dyed

It was greas: to make sope of

There was love, though, in the communal act of playing music. The aggregate sound from a large ensemble, the self, expanded, dendrite, axon—a magnificent multicellular creature (each person, each instrument section), like a colony of coral, and orchestra and choral, it evolves into an ecosystem of sound.
Love, then love for the culmination and synergy—

Can you love what you cannot see?

Start with a bar, a phrase. A few notes together in your hand. The curtains rise, linger in the lift, deflate—

The world's blurry when you're not in it.

I doe veryly: beleev: s'd Ann Puddeater is a: wich

I am already home—

ANN SPEAKS

I should be gathering sunlight. Skin lit with morning. Strands of hair falling to my cheek, tucked behind the ear. An unbroken horizon over the forest, past that, the sea, the sea, then England. I have an equally damp heart as before, feet on a different soil. So give me sun. My mouth is open, my hands cold. My throat's exposed. I hear coyote and wolf and bobcat, but when the night has left again, finch and thrush fill my ears.

Give me a reason to lift my gaze. My exhales keep arriving. My footprints line the path, mud speckles my ankles. A breeze now, salting my clothes. Blackbirds calling from the reeds.

How foolish I was to think I could so quickly return to polished stone—

WHAT'S LOST, WHAT'S FOUND

Like clothes on the floor, the scatterings of what's lost and what's found:

A winged maple seed, a snapped off second hand, cherry blossomed sidewalks, step by step by step.

The sun getting hotter by the minute.

Hop once, throw the stone, hop over, stone now warm in your palm, turn back, still balanced on one leg.

A bleeding hangnail, a paper cut, weeping alone in the bath.

The first green of trees, a zigzag line of tulips, cardinals calling tirelessly into the rain.

The smallest bones of the ear (stapes, incus, malleus), and fingertips loaded with nerves.

I am gathering it all:

Black petals, feathers, sun off the creek, a felt hat, a gesture (blinking), a rasping lieder, a maroon velvet cape, tadpoles, new pennies, pieces of grosgrain, leather laces, brass grommets, pressed queen anne's lace, a gentle wave, silver hoop earrings, a baby tooth, an old wrinkled map, grass clippings, sand from a shoe, fresh tea leaves, goodbyes, handshakes, yeps, yawns, hellos, aspirin (acetylsalicylic acid), sneezes, hoof polish, hairbrush, keepsakes, goodness sakes, sake, teaspoons, sleep.

AT THE PRECIPICE OF THE HELD NOTE

"Bella by Barlight," John Lurie

From the start, you have to lean in to listen—plucked strings open against and through the silence, three notes, then three more. *Largo*, a somnolent near-shuffle phrasing: a half note, followed by two quarters—in harmonics. It's almost out the range of your hearing, the musicians etching the piece out of the air. As if there were fog, as if they were fog. A steady progression against, a song of shadow, hazed light, the feel of a silk dress brushing against your arm, a glint of glassware reflected in your eye, sliver of blue sky through a cracked door.

Your heartbeat slows, listening, the piece gaining ground, a soft scrabble forward by repetition of hushed phrasing. Then, half way through, an abrupt crescendo—you startle a little—the leap from harmonics to full, true bowed notes. But still, you have to crane your neck closer to the speaker—under it all, is there a held note—a viola?

The volume drops away like it previously poured in, an afterthought, a circling backward, a drift into a dusky evening. Like a slow, retreating train, off along the horizon—dropped into *pianissimo*, then *pianississimo*—a conversation whispered, almost discerned—

MIGRATIONS
#7804

Wolf 7804: two year-old, 60 pound female radio-collared, wanderer, *disperser*, in search of a mate:

> Six months, a 2,593 mile loop (301 mile radius) from Minnesota into Wisconsin, 5 mph, 12 hrs/day, most of the miles covered in 72 days, only to return 25 miles from her birthplace. Crossed major highways 215 times.
>
> Cut collar found buried in mud, animal assumed dead.

IT'S NOT CLEAR IF IT'S A RIFT OR A RISING

In this fathom-long body with its perceptions and thoughts
there is the world, the origin of the world, the ending
of the world and the path to the ending of the world.

The Buddha

What Celia imagines most about the cellist is the smell of her skin, a combination of faint coffee beans, the crisp pages of a new notebook. The almost invisible moisture that seeps into her pores during a walk, her hair wet with mist.

No, maybe it's more flour and a touch of fresh soil, and salt, of course, and what's that?—longing?

She would tuck her face into the soft curve of her forearm and inhale. Yes, that's it, my dear. You.

But never mind. Mind instead in insatiable dread that lays its fat hand on her sternum each morning when she wakes. The noisome gravity of anxiety, a speeding and tripping heart. It's no use. She has long forgotten the rest.

Ineluctable, insatiable, unmoored—

One rests hope in the hearts of others.

What then, then? What sphere of understanding, what plane thick with concrete pleasures—a ripe tangerine, a daisy held by the stem, wood smoke in your hair?

The adrenaline, your own factory of rev and spin and go, churning, churning, churning.

There are ways. Yes, there are many ways.

—w—

How can one be lonely, within your own body? As if there's a rift in the ladder of DNA, you've slipped between the rungs of the paired bases, tumbled into something simple yet undefined, fuzzy-edged. The absence of serotonin and dopamine, the faltering neurotransmitters, sparse, your heart dulled, your arms heavy?

Can one overlook the histories her genes contain? The silent, the unexpressed—

It's a gentleness, to love your genome (shut your eyes: the family tree with squares and circles, the branching backward of ancestors, some with names underneath, some with question marks. Others without birthdays. A few fade away from the future.)

At the same time, the bright, hot stars linger, firing biochemical pathways, cells churning, dividing, manufacturing, dying—Tell me, telomere, how long can we last?

—w—

The murmurations of starlings, a skein of geese

—~—

I woke up to gold outside—the maples suddenly in full amber-flare, and a windy night carpeted the neighbor's large front lawn and mine, too, with leaves—so the muted light today is enough to set the street aglow, a web of yellow, a wet leaf stuck to the bedroom window—and now with the sun behind the trees, it's like having a candle inside a pumpkin, or the color sensed inside your chest when you wake up to such a beautiful ochre atmosphere (no, more of a saffron)—you can't help but feel illuminated, and about to burst.

—~—

The blue eye of a fledgling crow and the blue eye of the ibis—a human baby's blue eye, ephemeral—the sky reflected back—

—~—

Grey clouds are moving quickly to the northeast, white clouds higher up—a few raindrops. The frilled petticoated edges of pink hollyhocks and their darker centers. A hummingbird flies by as loud as a large bee. In a dusk-dark room, breeze to your face, crickets marking time with their sawing limbs, leaves acting like leaves in the wind, the bare limbs of winter beneath.

—~—

What happens when it's the hour of lead, as Dickinson writes, upon you, unasked, the noise of the world?

—~—

Simultaneous, sun in your eye, sun in your ear, in the strands of your hair, tendrils (locket, keepsake, keep-safe, heart)—there was never a moment of solitude, rustling leaves, solar flare against the sternum (the thousands of ways to unravel—) The tide of ( ), the tide of *I nevers*— Out of the corner of the eye, like living with a ghost, an invisible twin, a hint, a shadow, a whispered namesake—

Whenever there is a moment, a single breath (exhale)— Nothing. Axons and dendrites, the innate electricity, unnoticed. The buzz of radio static. Late night highway, flash of the white lines blurring, just as your thoughts spark and smear early in the morning when little moves, when so much breathes so softly, even the stars. The tide, spread to the middle of the continent—wheat fields, a flock of gathering blackbirds, once, again alights—

—~—

Attempt to access the inaccessible: a long nap, a savored cup of tea, giving in, cantilevering between breath and death, between awake and submerged, singular versus multi-focal, recalibrating, rejecting the flurried tasks—

—~—

Walking the dog in sort of a leash-pulling trance, and then later, the four a.m. insomnia, whenever, whatever, that placeless shelter of sleep (come back). This body, your body. Look into your dog's eyes—

And when did we falter?

—~—

The hours are not expansive enough to accommodate—

—~—

What was missing for Celia was silence—to still the machinery in her head, retract from the surface noise of the street and man-made air's cacophony, each taut muscle released— The closest, palpable territory was an exhausted afternoon nap, bird trill in the periphery, light amongst leaves shifting across the bed, closed eyelids.

Returning: a dog bark, a spoon set on a plate, a car door, a yell down the street.

—~—

The thick, undisturbed sleep of a medicated night—almost, an inescapable room; no, it's not contained, you wouldn't even call it velvet-dense or syrup-thick, liquid or solid, or even oxygenated. No lingering in the almost-sleep town, more like a light switch *off.* Perhaps the dead live here. Maybe her deceased, wholly perfect, wholly missed, good dog of a decade, maybe he's here, too.

She doesn't remember anything from her hours asleep; maybe she's not anywhere to be found except the fact that her heart beats and she keeps breathing during this absence. It begins to feel as if someone else is in charge. Someone elses, plural? (pleural) A line in the energetic spectrum of being, of what's capable and culpable is of no matter, a flurry of loss, a loss of intention, a void of comprehensible word. An energetic uncoupling, a stasis, a scent of ? (soundless). How and where. Whether we leave at all. Whether we return. Each night, a slivering—

—~—

As if dissociation from now is merely an association with an other, a connectivity with possibility.

—~—

Darker out, and darker still. (How quiet it was then, before.)

Matter is neither created nor destroyed (oh, souls—). An object in motion stays in motion (oh, loss—). For every action, there is an equal an opposite reaction (oh, birth—).

The friction of so many voices, guttered, heat dissipating— No matter. (Dark matter, a spark, the universe.) No matter. (I have loved.) I have worked a gentle angle. Even after holding one's body taut for years.

—~—

Multitudinous, unfolding—

The timid, early hour, crickets scattering their trills, the moon a lingering scent—

—~—

Monocyte, mollusk, molecular, metropolis, monotreme, monument.

Mal-aligned. Maligned.

—~—

Look up!, Rilke and Whitman, might say, *Look up! and live!* But it's not the poets commanding your attention: instead, it's a sign tacked to a telephone pole, electric lines cut for road construction.

Look up—the sumacs are torched by fall, exuberance before sleep.

—∾—

For those of us more comfortable around animals than humans, does this mean our reincarnations are askew? Or maybe they were purposeful, and we're that link to everything animate, the ones that remind us that anthropomorphism is just one viewpoint, that there are others.

So easily we can forget about the sparrows along the roof gutters, the whales sounding through the oceans.

—∾—

She had a strata of kindness(es), earthen, unknown

—∾—

And in the eyes of others around you, what's that rustling below the surface?

THE WORLD WITHIN

Stop, wait. Listen to the shift of the tree limbs against each other, the scuttling of insect legs, the quiet, heliotropic turnings of flowers. A song comes through the sternum, the world within, the word without.

Four strings, a bow. The sounds erupt, unravel, unspool, manifest, accelerate, tumult. Heart under the ribcage, bones like a tuning fork. What we return for, despite our failings, our sloughage. The dozens of muscles choreographed, a flurry of fingers, a memory imprint out of vapor into tone, so that there may be a form for joy, for sadness, for disparity, for unity.

The options are endless, like the restless need for stories—a musician, through spark and chance and luck, takes the world in her hands, and in return—notes towards—

She cannot give up. Yes, the cello's case gathers dusk in the crease and teeth of the zipper. Yes, the strings go slack and out of tune with lack of use. But having the beast behind the door, waiting, she never forgets. Her home where no one is asking anything from her, and scales and song flutter out the window to whomever is listening.

She is the only one asking anything. Her heart can be harsh (she has forgotten most of what made her a good musician).

But then, remembering the heft of the wood in her hands—she cannot imagine her life without it.

What it would be to stop, to search for what, to replace the lost? The quiet key in the lock, the oak animal disappeared, a horsehair found behind the dresser as a reminder. Rosin-sticky.

THAT BLUE IN THE PERIPHERY

When she wakes, the first thing she hears is the wind in the trees. If the wind is down, then the waves, against the red rocks of the shoreline. It is the utter lack of human racket that strikes her, while she is still sleepy, the absence of traffic, voices, car doors, front doors, or dogs (besides her own ghost's). She feels herself unspooling stress after a few days of listening, waking slowly, and her posture straightens, her chest broadens, and she sleeps more soundly.

And yet, after a few days, after a week, after a month, she must return home. She goes back to the landscape of human clatter and few moments of stillness, the remembered lives and work that she has built for herself.

The lake, the aspens, the blue tongue of the waves all start to evaporate, and she picks up her cell phone, checks her email, and turns on the tv. Maybe even her misanthropy rears its head again—there is always someone else in front of you, no matter where you go.

When she is not too entrenched in the A to B trajectory, if she sits in her car for one moment longer, hands to the wheel and she looks up at the sky, she may come to the conclusion, *This is not working out for me.*

Yes, there are Thai and Jamaican restaurants near her house, an intricate byway of bike paths, and prairie gardens of native plants in some of her neighbors' yards. But she can't stop feeling like she can't fully inflate her lungs.

She remembers, just last week, *I saw 10 pileated woodpeckers in three days.*

But it is not as if her hours away were devoid of all other human-made noises. A car driving down the gravel road, the sound of a hammer far off, voices on the water from a boat, the phone ringing. No matter, at home, she finds a legion of excuses to prevent her from attending to her core's quiet refueling.

There is just so much talking, so much static caroming around inside her skull, that everything feels tangled, knotted.

But don't we just take our burdens from place to place?

So then, how long can you hang onto that smooth stone once you return to where you left off?

PETITION

The humble Petition of Ann Poodeater unto the honoured Judge and Bench now Setting in Judicature in Salem humbly Sheweth:

That Wheras your Poor and humble Petitioner being condemned to die and knowing in my own conscience as I shall shortly answer it before the great God of heaven who is the searcher & knower of all hearts: That the Evidence of Jno Best Sen'r and Jno Best Jun'r and Sam'll Pickworth w'ch was given in against me in Court were all of them altogether false & untrue and besides the abovesaid Jno Best hath been formerly whipt and likewise is rcorded for a Lyar I would humbly begg of yo'r honours to Take it into your Judicious and Pious consideration That my life may not be taken away by such false Evidence and wittnesses as these be likewise the Evidence given in against me by Sarah Church and Mary Warren I am altogether ignorant off and know nothing in the least measure about it nor nothing else concerning the crime of witchcraft for w'ch I am condemned to die as will be known to men and angells att the great day of Judgment begging and imploring your prayers att the throne of grace in my behalfe and your poor and humble petition'r shall for ever pray as she is bound in duty for your hon'rs health and happiness in this life and eternall felicity in the world to come

BLACKBIRD SKY

I can barely tell apart the birds from leaves in my neighbor's yard, yet thousands of blackbirds just settled there, disappearing into the foliage. The dusk sky crowds low rain clouds together, where shades of grey push and blur against each other. Looking at the tops of my neighbor's maples, I see silhouettes of individual birds if I look carefully, if I squint.

Yet I can't tell how many trees have birds in them because their silhouettes act as mirages. My eyes strain and falter, focus and fail. But the noise quantifies. A cacophony of birds pop and call and creak, the discord of chiming and chattering broken occasionally by an individual whistling a few discernible notes, clear as a town crier. One clear voice gives locality to the confusion.

I'm on my front porch across the street from the birds, and all I can do is stare. I don't know where the birds come from or how they find each other and form a large flock like this. But it is as if all the birds in this valley have settled their black bodies to talk on my street.

The clamor gets in my veins, straight from the blood vessels in my eardrums to my extremities. It's shrill and uncomfortable. Slightly sinister, warbling like the end of the a.m. dial.

The birds come in two waves, one right after the other, before settling among the trees. This blackbird surf gets me imagining the clouds of passenger pigeons that blackened the sky before extinction. For a half a second, I feel like I'm at the turn of the century, wings blotting out the sun as the rumble and scrape of millions of brown doves' wings fill my ears. It's hard to breathe, my eyes and ears saturated with flight stop my lungs, so I choke. I cough back feathers and risen dirt. But I am awed as a mass of pigeons flies by, leaving me behind in their trail of lost feathers.

The blackbirds overhead hover in the sky in an indecipherable Braille, a whole novel of black dots spilled into the sky, shifting. The birds advance as elastic, a school in the sky, moving as a group, leaderless, a joint mind directing them. Away, right, left, down, up. Few falter or stray. The group is tight as careful choreography. They lull me, pushing into my unconscious, so when I sleep I see them as a cloud of feathers sweeping against another, against my eyelids and torso and arms.

I stand under a tree and it shivers and shimmies with blackbirds rustling their feathers, feathers falling down to dust the street like the gift from some random but dreamy god.

As the flock waits for whatever they wait for, stragglers pass over the tops of the trees picking up and losing members. The flock originally moved in from the southwest, all birds traveling in one direction, down the street, along the line of trees, northward. Now another smaller flock pushes in, stalling above the tree with the most birds. Then the new group splits in half and goes in opposite directions. The rest lands three trees down.

The blackbirds are grouping and slowly proceeding along my street, not going south, but in the opposite direction that they need to travel to stay warm and alive for the winter. But they only advance northward for a block.

Some bird species use the sun as a compass during the day. Or others guide themselves at night with Polaris and other stars and constellations. Perhaps the birds are in my neighborhood to rest and wait for the sky to clear after the residual rain of a hurricane gone inland. When the sky clears, little receptors in their thousands of similarly programmed brains point to the

North Star. The birds will look up and orient themselves south by it. More than I can do. I can hardly get up the stairs of my house in the dark.

The blackbirds on my street probably also recognize certain natural landmarks like rivers and vistas, and perhaps, the unnatural, like freeways and the capitol. Do they think, when they come back in the spring, Oh, we are almost Home—there's the stadium, the parking lots, and now I can rest?

Their brains are also rigged to pick up magnetic fields in mountains ranges. Imagine it, feeling the pull of metals in the ground, rivers of hidden iron ore acting as a map. When the cloud cover gets low, just fly according the pulse and pull of the ions you cannot see.

Oh, *Zugunruhe:* the birds on my street are definitely fidgety, hopping from tree to tree before their long trip.

In less than a minute after landing on a communal roost, the blackbirds alight in an upward thrust like one large wing. It's the suddenness and the sound I can't shake loose. The jabbering stops and thousands of pairs of wings amplify the updraft, a mass of feather and bone and muscle moving in unison. All the hearts beat quickly in a fast tempoed scherzo, the metronome of their knocking overlapping and deafening to the ears of animals more specialized than humans.

As the birds leave, I gasp, surprise sucked out of me by the immediate and unexpected *whoosh.* The birds prattled just seconds earlier as if they were satisfied with their temporary home, content to gossip and fret and plan about the journey ahead. Then they are up, wings open, sending them down the street on some unspoken and invisible clue. As quickly as my breath is dragged out of me, as fast as I jump, I am also unhappy to be left behind, flightless, like failure, stuck in one ground-bound point of view.

What it must feel like to pick up and fly amid the noise and clutter, among the beautiful motion of countless birds, small dark eyes filled with black bodies, almost brushing nearby wings, the notion of *go* and *move* the only thing in the brain, all tapped into the mantra of migration, the shorter days somehow saying *find others like you.* In the birds' restlessness, there is excitement. On the ground, then suddenly, up.

I can almost get there with them, the original flock near the creek now:

From the trees, they see sheep in the nearby fields. The black backs of calves and their mothers shine on the hill, a quartet of horses jostles near the dairy. The highway weaves over the land a half mile away, the string of headlights flashing against the hills. For the moment, they are content just to warble and move from limb to limb, the blood in their bodies revving for the feat ahead.

SOURCES

Italicized right-side justified texts, as well as other italicized court documents, are from the website: "Salem Witch Trials: Documentary Archive and Transcription Project," (http://etext.virginia.edu/salem/witchcraft/texts/transcripts.html) copyright 2003, by the Rector and Visitors of the University of Virginia, based upon *The Salem Witchcraft Papers, Volume 3: Verbatim Transcripts of the Legal Documents of the Salem Witchcraft Outbreak of 1692*, edited and with an introduction and notes by Paul Boyer and Stephen Nissenbaum.

6 The quote comes from the liner notes to the Kronos Quartet's *Ghost Opera*

27 The quote by Nevins is from Daniel Lang's "Poor Ann!," *The New Yorker*, Sept. 11, 1954

29 The quote from the article is from the website, http://www.usgs.gov/newsroom/article.asp?ID=443

33 A blue whale's heart the size of a VW Bug is from: http://www.coolantarctica.com/Antarctica%20fact%20file/wildlife/whales/blue_whale.htm

"An average blue is about the equivalent of about 25 fully grown African bull elephants. Another way of looking at it is that an elephant is to a blue whale as a rabbit is to a human."

33 Italicized text is from Tu Fu's "Drinking There Alone," in *Carrying Over*, trans. by Carolyn Kizer

37 The concept "transcending death through progeny" comes from Laurel Thatcher Ulrich, *Goodwives: Image and Reality of Lives of Women in Northern New England 1650-1750*

38–39 The quote is from Daniel Lang's "Poor Ann!" *The New Yorker*, Sept. 11, 1954

50 Directions to Gallows Hill is from the website, http://www.salemwitchmuseum.com/tour/salem.shtml

55 The story of the young captured great white is from the website, http://www.mbayaq.org/cr/whiteshark.asp

61 Italicized text in quotes is from *Essex County Archives, Salem — Witchcraft Vol. 2*

62 Text in quotes comes from "He Wants Her Name Cleared: Judd's Ancestor Killed as a Witch," newspaper article, source unknown, xeroxed as a source in my brother Mark's Honors English Period 7 paper, "The Greenslit Family Tree," ~ circa mid to later 1970s

62 Text in quotes is by Daniel Lang, "Poor Ann!" *The New Yorker*, Sept. 11, 1954

65 Information on Humphrey the whale comes from the websites, http://en.wikipedia.org/wiki/Marine_Mammal_Center and http://en.wikipedia.org/wiki/Humphrey_the_Whale

67 Definition of ergot is from Encarta® World English Dictionary © 1999 Microsoft Corporation, for Microsoft by Bloomsbury Publishing Plc.

67–68 Text in italics is from the website, http://www.pbs.org/wnet/secrets/case_salem/clues.html

73 Epigraph is from "The Tower Beyond Tragedy," *The Selected Poetry of Robinson Jeffers*

81 Epigraph is from Mazzy Star's "Into Dust," recorded on *So Tonight That I Might See*

84 The concept of the ghost bird is by Jonathan Rosen, "The Ghost Bird," *The New Yorker*, May 14, 2001

85–86 Text in quotes is from the book of Genesis

87 Text is quotes is by Dogen Zenji, from Joan Halifax, *The Fruitful Darkness: Reconnecting with the Body of the Earth*

89 Text in quotes is by Ted Hall, from the website, acupuncturetoday.com, April 2001

91 Text in quotes is from Tu Fu's "A Visit in Winter to the Temple of His Mystical Majesty," in *Carrying Over*, trans. by Carolyn Kizer

93 Text in quotes is from Tu Fu's "Thwarted," in *Carrying Over*, trans. by Carolyn Kizer

94 Text in quotes is by Sogyal Rinpoche, *The Tibetan Book of Living and Dying*

103 The song, "Bella By Barlight" was recorded on *Winter Was Hard*, Kronos Quartet

105 The information on the wolf's travels is based on Darlene Pfister's "Dispatches from a Lone Wolf," *Star Tribune*, April 5, 2000

107 Epigraph from *Anguttara Nikaya*, 4:451